Getting-to-Grandad Bears

written by Hiawyn Oram
with pictures by Frédéric Joos

A

Andersen Press • London

Big Bear and Baby Bear were in the train on their way to visit Grandad.

"Are we nearly there yet?" said Baby Bear.

Text copyright © 2001 by Hiawyn Oram. Illustrations copyright © 2001 by Frédéric Joos
The rights of Hiawyn Oram and Frédéric Joos to be identified as the author and illustrator of this
work have been asserted by them in accordance with the Copyright, Designs and Patents Act, 1988.
First published in Great Britain in 2001 by Andersen Press Ltd., 20 Vauxhall Bridge Road,
London SW1V 2SA. Published in Australia by Random House Australia Pty.,
20 Alfred Street, Milsons Point, Sydney, NSW 2061. All rights reserved.
Colour separated in Italy by Fotoriproduzioni Grafiche, Verona.
Printed and bound in Italy by Grafiche AZ, Verona.

10   9   8   7   6   5   4   3   2   1

British Library Cataloguing in Publication Data available.

ISBN 1 84270 010 3

This book has been printed on acid-free paper

"No, no!" said Big Bear. "It's a long way and takes a long time to get to Grandad's."

"Then what shall we do to make it go faster?" said Baby Bear.

"Have some sandwiches," said Big Bear.
So Baby Bear ate some sandwiches and when
they were finished she licked her paws slowly.

"Are we nearly there *now?*" she said.

"No, no!" said Big Bear. "Not even nearly."

"Then what else shall we do to make it go faster?" said Baby Bear.

"Colouring-in," said Big Bear. So Baby Bear coloured in and joined the dots and coloured in some more and joined some more dots.

When everything was coloured in and all the dots joined, she put the tops back on her pens slowly.

"Are we nearly there *now?*" she said.

"No, no!" said Big Bear. "Not even half way!"

"Then what ELSE shall we do to make it go faster?" said Baby Bear.

"Read a story," said Big Bear.
So Baby Bear climbed onto Big Bear's lap and Big Bear read and Baby Bear listened and so did everyone else in their compartment.

When the story was finished Baby Bear closed the book slowly.

"Are we nearly there NOW?" she said.

"Uh . . . just past half way," said Big Bear.

"Then what CAN we do to get there faster?" said Baby Bear.

"Sleep?" said Big Bear, yawning.

"Sleep!" cried Baby Bear. "Much too slow!"
Then she jumped off Big Bear's lap and ran up
the corridor . . .

and down again . . .

and up again . . .

and down and up again . . .

and out of the way of two Big Dogs . . .

and up again . . . and down again . . . until a
Baby Rabbit popped up and asked if he could
join her.

And they ran together . . . up the corridor . . .

and down again . . .

and up into a corner to whisper their secrets . . .

and down again . . . and out of the way of a
bad-tempered Big Pig . . .

and up again . . . and down again . . . and up again . . .
until they ran slap bang into the conductor.

"Whoops!" he said. "Better get back to your seats . . . because you know what? We're coming into the station!"

"See!" said Baby Bear running back to Big Bear. "What?" said Big Bear, opening the eye she was dozing with. "Are we nearly there?"

"Not *nearly!*" said Baby Bear. "We're THERE!"

"Right here!" said Grandad coming in to help with the luggage and picking up Baby Bear and kissing her and hugging her. "Have you had a long journey?"

"Oh no!" said Baby Bear. "'Cos I kept on running so we got here FASTER!"